IMPORTANT NOTICE

The rebels have destroyed the Death Star! Darth Vader has to inform the Emperor using his holoprojector. Find his password by searching for a set of unique symbols that don't appear in any other combination.

> MAYBE WE SHOULDN'T CALL HIM? WE CAN BUILD A NEW DEATH STAR. THE EMPEROR WON'T EVEN NOTICE . . .

CODE 1

CODE 2

CODE 3

CODE 4

CODE 5

A NEW HOPE

When the Emperor first heard of the most powerful weapon in the galaxy —
the legendary Kyber Saber — he wanted to get his hands on it. It would be
quite useful in the fight against the rebels after losing the Death Star!

> MASTER, I HAVE SENT OUR
> BEST AGENT IN SEARCH OF
> THE KYBER SABER CRYSTALS.

The Kyber Saber is so powerful that its maker broke the crystal blade and hid its pieces in various locations across the galaxy. Can you piece them back together? Place the fragments in the appropriate positions.

4

3

6

1

5

2

7

EXCELLENT, LORD VADER. I WANT IT AS FAST AS POSSIBLE! PREFERABLY BEFORE DINNER!

THE FREEMAKERS

Welcome to the space station known as "the Wheel"! Here you'll find the salvage and repair shop owned by the Freemakers, a family of galactic junk collectors. While they're looking for a super important starship part, can you try to discover their names?

Although he is the youngest of the three siblings, he discovered the Force within himself.

The sister running the family business. She can sell any piece of junk, with a profit!

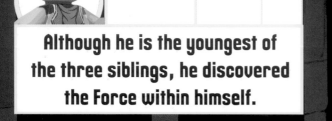

R

GE

KO

RO

Look at the pile below and find bricks of the same colors that match the frames with the descriptions of the characters. Then put them in order from the largest to the smallest and write the letters on them into the empty boxes to read the names.

The eldest of the three. None can match his starship repair skills!

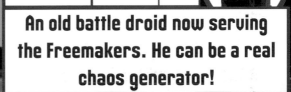

An old battle droid now serving the Freemakers. He can be a real chaos generator!

R

N

ZAN

DE

DI

RO

R

WA

JEDI AND THE BEAST

When Rowan used the Force and found the first fragment of the Kyber Saber hidden inside a cave, he was attacked by an enormous dianoga! Luckily, a Jedi in hiding named Naare was close by. Guide her through the maze so she can save the boy from the attacking beast!

EW! BRUSH YOUR TEETH BEFORE ATTACKING SOMEONE!

RENOVATION

Zander loves tinkering, especially with his beloved special purpose starship — the *StarScavenger*!

Help Kordi figure out the cost of the renovation by marking eight parts of the starship Zander fiddled with.

JEDI TRAINING

Naare agreed to help Rowan master the Force, but first she needs him to prepare the training field. Place five practice dummies on the grid, so that there is at least one empty space between each dummy.

A BIT TO THE LEFT. A BIT MORE . . . NOT THIS LEFT, THE OTHER LEFT . . . YOU KNOW WHAT? THAT LEFT WAS ACTUALLY RIGHT.

A BUMPY SITUATION

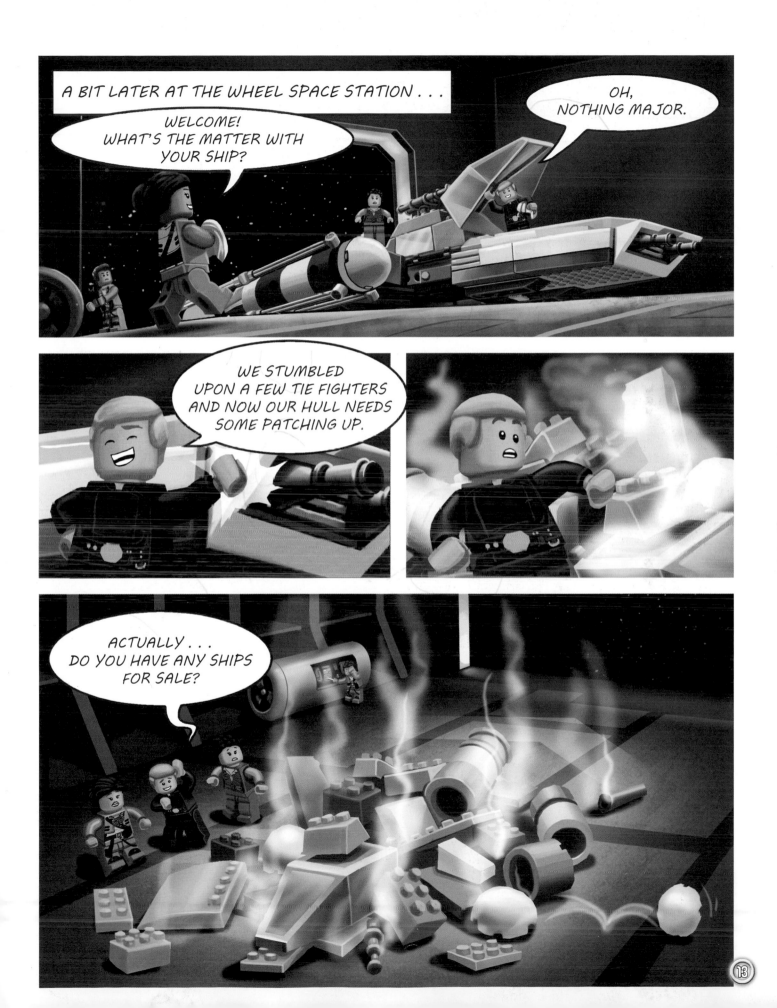

LET THEM SHOOT!

Why look for junk in far corners of the galaxy? You can just hide out near a space battle. Just wait a little while and junk will gather itself for you! Once you finish gazing at the battling starfighters, look at the parts in the box and mark the spots on the starships they come from.

NO WAY! WE'LL GET PAID WELL FOR THE PARTS WE CAN COLLECT HERE!

KORDI, SHOULDN'T WE BE WAITING A LITTLE BIT FARTHER AWAY?

TRAINING WITH THE MASTER

Rowan just received a few tips from Luke Skywalker — this is training worthy of a Jedi! Now it's time to see if he can make use of them. Knowing Luke's attacks, put appropriate defense symbols inside the empty spaces and help Rowan learn how to quickly counter attacks.

ATTACKS:

К	thrust
Ϟ	cut from the left
↓	cut from the right
Ц	cut from the top

DEFENSE:

Ϡ	against cuts from the right
↑	against the cut from the top
↙	against thrusts
Ϟ	against cuts from the left

KORDI'S SYSTEM

Being the head of the family business, Kordi created her own system for keeping tools in the workshop. To others, it seems like a total mess, but it actually makes sense to her. Place the missing tools on the rack by writing their assigned letters inside the blank squares. Remember that no tool can appear more than once in any column or row.

A

B

C

D

SHALL I TIDY UP A BIT?

DON'T YOU DARE! I CAN'T FIND MY TOOLS IN A NEAT WORKSHOP!

BUSINESS IS BUSINESS

Kordi just received valuable information about derelict ships drifting in a faraway asteroid field. Help the Freemakers get to them by writing down the coordinates of sectors containing rocks identical to the one in the picture. Don't let anyone get there before the siblings.

KORDI, WE DON'T HAVE TIME FOR THIS! THE GALAXY NEEDS SAVING!

OH, IT WILL ONLY TAKE A MINUTE. I EVEN HAVE A BUYER FOR THIS JUNK . . .

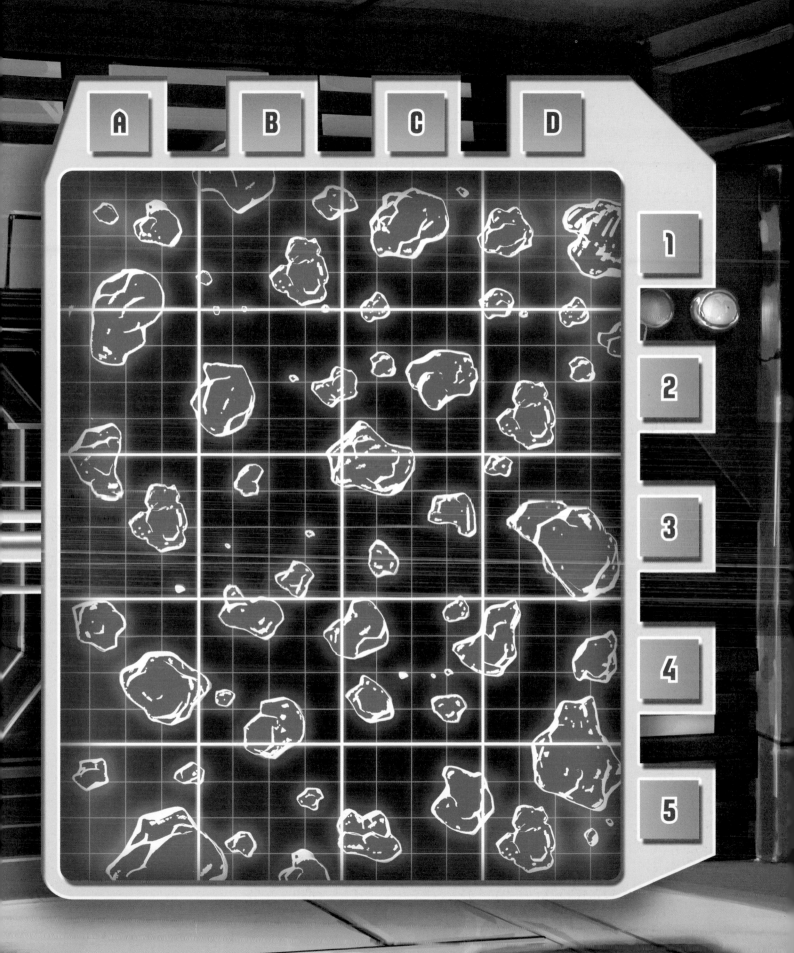

A B C D

1 2 3 4 5

A NEW DEATH STAR

SOMEWHERE IN A REMOTE CORNER OF THE GALAXY . . .

HOW IS THE WORK ON OUR NEW BATTLE STATION PROCEEDING?

WE ARE ALMOST DONE, LORD VADER.

I HOPE THE EMPEROR WILL BE PLEASED.

HE BETTER BE, FOR YOUR SAKE.

WE GAVE IT OUR BEST. WE WANTED THE SECOND DEATH STAR TO BE IMPRESSIVE!

INDEED, THE FIRST IMPRESSION IS VERY IMPORTANT.

SIR, WE HAVE ARRIVED. BEHOLD, THE NEW DEATH STAR!

WE DECIDED TO ADD A BIT, LORD VADER. IMPRESSIVE, HUH?

I'M NOT SURE IF THIS IS THE IMPRESSION THE EMPEROR WANTS.

DOUBLE AGENT

Thanks to Rowan's affinity with the Force, Naare obtained all the crystals and rebuilt the Kyber Saber. But now she wants to take control over the galaxy herself! To achieve this, she will need to face one more foe. Who is this opponent? Untangle the lines to find out.

LET'S BUILD!

Rowan's control over the Force has become much better lately — he can even rebuild the *StarScavenger* without any tools! To make his job easier, look at the list of parts he'll need and mark the right sequences of the levitating bricks.

TAKE OUT TRASH. BUY PRESENT FOR ZANDER. FIND THE KYBER SABER CRYSTALS . . . OOPS, WRONG LIST.

A

B

C

D

A NEW TEACHER

Rowan has a new master — JEK-14! Under his teacher's watchful eye, he is learning how to build with the Force. Today's assignment: Use the Force to locate the correct spare part in the pile . . . with closed eyes. Help Rowan locate the part — it's the only one without a match!

HURRY UP. WE DON'T HAVE ALL DAY! THERE ARE 34 OTHER EXERCISES FOR YOU TO DO.

I JUST HOPE ONE OF THEM IS TAKING A NAP!

A CUNNING PLAN

Now in control of the powerful Kyber Saber, Naare is on her way to the Emperor's palace. To get there, Rowan decided to disguise himself as Palpatine. Help him choose the best costume by marking the one most similar to the Emperor's robes from the picture.

A

B

C

D

E

F

G

H

INFILTRATING THE EMPEROR'S PALACE AND RECOVERING THE STRONGEST WEAPON IN THE GALAXY . . . NOT EXACTLY A JOB FOR A 12-YEAR-OLD!

ESCAPE

Rowan managed to retrieve the Kyber Saber! Help him escape the Emperor's palace while hiding from Naare and the Emperor. Choose the steps according to the color sequence given in the template and draw an escape route leading to his brother and sister.

QUIZ

1. What is the name of the most powerful weapon in the galaxy?
   A. Kyber Saber
   B. Casper Saber
   C. Carpet Saber

2. What is the profession of the Freemaker family?
   A. Sale of expensive footwear
   B. Junk collecting and starship repair
   C. Space catering

3. Who saved Rowan from the giant dianoga?
   A. Naare
   B. Roger
   C. Darth Vader

4. Which one of the Freemaker siblings is Force-sensitive?
   A. Rowan
   B. Zander
   C. Kordi

5. Which well-known Jedi did Rowan meet on the Wheel?
   A. Qui-Gon Jinn
   B. Luke Skywalker
   C. Obi-Wan Kenobi

6. Zander specializes in:
   A. Programming droids
   B. Repairing starships
   C. Vegetarian grills

7. Naare is actually:
   A. A bounty hunter
   B. A thief
   C. A Sith agent

ANSWERS

Pg. 1 IMPORTANT NOTICE

CODE 5

Pgs. 6–7 JEDI AND THE BEAST

Pgs. 2–3 A NEW HOPE

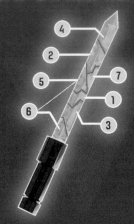

Pgs. 8–9 RENOVATION

Pgs. 4–5 THE FREEMAKERS

RO WA N
KO R DI
ZAN DE R
RO GE R

Pgs. 10–11 JEDI TRAINING

Pgs. 14–15 LET THEM SHOOT!

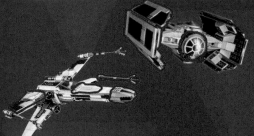

Pg. 17 KORDI'S SYSTEM

Pgs. 18–19 BUSINESS IS BUSINESS

B1, D2, A3, D5

Pg. 16 TRAINING WITH THE MASTER

Pg. 21 DOUBLE AGENT

Pgs. 22–23 LET'S BUILD!

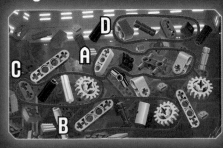

Pg. 24 A NEW TEACHER

Pg. 25 A CUNNING PLAN

G

Pgs. 26–27 ESCAPE

Pgs. 28–29 STAR QUIZ

1A, 2B, 3A, 4A, 5B, 6B, 7C

HOW TO BUILD
A DEATH STAR TROOPER
MINIFIGURE